MW00907860

Danny at the Car Wash

written and photographed
by
Mia Coulton

Dad got a new car.

Dad put Bee on the roof.

"Look," said Dad.

"My new car

has a sunroof.

Can you see

the sunroof, Bee?"

"Oh no," said Dad.

"Look at my new car.

My new car is dirty.

Let's go to the car wash."

Off we go to the car wash.

"Here we go
into the car wash.
Don't be scared, Danny,"
said Dad.

"Here comes the water. Don't be scared, Danny," said Dad.

"Here comes the soap. Don't be scared, Danny," said Dad.

"Here comes Bee!

Oh, no!

Don't be scared, Bee!

Hold on!" screamed Dad.

The new car is clean
and so is Bee.

Dad said to Bee, "You need to ride inside the car. You need to be safe."

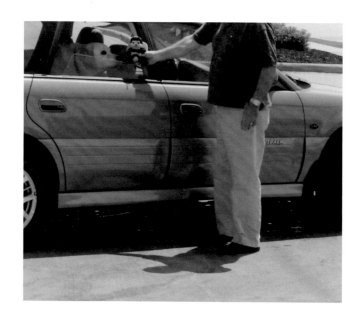